Christmas
Gifts

Christmas
Gifts

by Susan Heyboer O'Keefe

Illustrated by Jennifer Emery

Boyds Mills Press

Text copyright © 2004 by Susan Heyboer O'Keefe
Illustrations copyright © 2004 by Jennifer Emery

Published by Boyds Mills Press, Inc.
A Highlights Company
815 Church Street
Honesdale, Pennsylvania 18431
Printed in China

Library of Congress Cataloging-in-Publication Data

O'Keefe, Susan Heyboer.
Christmas gifts / Susan Heyboer O'Keefe ;
illustrated by Jennifer Emery.— 1st ed.
p.   cm.
Summary: Describes, in rhyming text and illustrations, all the
preparations that are made to celebrate Christmas.
ISBN 1-59078-083-3 (alk. paper)
[1. Christmas—Fiction. 2. Stories in rhyme.]
I. Emery, Jennifer, ill. II. Title.

PZ8.3.O37Ch 2004
[E]—dc22
2003026792

First edition, 2004
The text of this book is set in 28-point Optima.
Illustrations are done in watercolor.
Visit our Web site at www.boydsmillspress.com

10 9 8 7 6 5 4 3 2 1

For Carol Behrman,
Wonderful Writer, Wonderful Friend,
Wonderful Gift to Us All
—S. H. OK

To Mark
—J. E.

Christmas Eve,
I believe!
Hopeful looks
at snowy eave.

Tree is trimmed,
lights are dimmed.

Prayers are said
and carols hymned.

Not a peep!
Try to sleep.
Curiosity
will keep.

Christmas flight.
Wondrous sight!
Miracle of
pure delight!

Walls are stormed,
house transformed.

Silent sleeping hearts
are warmed.

Stockings fill,
boxes spill.
Love and joy
and all goodwill.

Christmas morn, Christ is born!

Play the harp, and play the horn!

Straw is piled.
Lay the child.
Ox and cow
have sweetly smiled.

Everywhere,
gifts to share.
Each reflecting
God's own care.

Christmas day—
Shout hooray!
Friends and family
on their way.

Steeple bells,
cooking smells.

Stories
Uncle Eddie tells.

Laughter, cheer.
Kisses dear.
Hugs so tight,
they last all year.